THE
RULES HAVE
CHANGED

THE RULES HAVE CHANGED

Lesley Choyce

orca soundings

ORCA BOOK PUBLISHERS

Published in Canada and the United States in 2021 by Orca Book Publishers.
orcabook.com

Library and Archives Canada Cataloguing in Publication
Title: The rules have changed / Lesley Choyce.
Names: Choyce, Lesley, 1951– author.
Series: Orca soundings.
Description: Series statement: Orca soundings
Identifiers: Canadiana (print) 20200273825 | Canadiana (ebook) 20200273833 |
ISBN 9781459826823 (softcover) | ISBN 9781459826830 (PDF) |
ISBN 9781459826847 (EPUB)
Classification: LCC PS8555.H668 R85 2021 | DDC jc813/.54—dc23

Library of Congress Control Number: 2020939251

Summary: In this high-interest accessible novel for teen readers,
sixteen-year-old Blake Pendleton is surprised to learn, after three years
abroad, that things are very different at his school now.

Orca Book Publishers is committed to reducing the consumption
of nonrenewable resources in the making of our books. We make every
effort to use materials that support a sustainable future.

Orca Book Publishers gratefully acknowledges the support for its publishing
programs provided by the following agencies: the Government of Canada,
the Canada Council for the Arts and the Province of British Columbia
through the BC Arts Council and the Book Publishing Tax Credit.

Design by Ella Collier
Cover design by Ella Collier
Cover artwork by Getty Images/gremlin
Edited by Tanya Trafford

Printed and bound in Canada.

24 23 22 21 • 1 2 3 4

For Neil Peart: writer, drummer, friend

Chapter One

"The rules have changed."

That's the first thing I was told when I showed up on my first day back at school. *What rules?* I wanted to ask. *What kind of changes?* But I decided to say nothing and keep my mouth shut.

Why?

Well, because everything about the school freaked me out. The uniforms. The kids staring at those slim metallic phones. The look on everyone's faces. I can't quite explain it. Let's just say they looked stern and serious. I could tell I wasn't going to like this at all.

"Here," the pinch-faced man in the office said, handing me one of those phones. "Keep this with you at all times. Answer it when it rings. Follow the instructions."

"I don't need a phone," I said. I'd been out of the country for three years. I hadn't used a cell phone in all that time. My parents had a backup satellite phone on the boat, but it was only for emergencies. Fortunately we had never needed it.

"You do now," he said, slapping it into my hand. "It's required. And when you address any staff around here, you refer to them as 'sir' or 'miss.'"

I stared at the shiny metal device and felt its coldness in my hand. "Yes, sir," I said, feeling like I wanted to scream and run out the door. *Be cool*, I told myself. *You're going to have to adjust, adapt. Learn to live back in the world you left behind.*

"Room 303," Sir said. "Political science. Tell Mr. King you are new. Tell him you are going to need training."

Training? What the hell? Was I some kind of dog?

"And be sure to come back and pick up your uniform at noon."

What was with the uniforms? I'd seen all the kids in khaki shirts and black pants—both boys and girls. I figured a lot had changed while I'd been gone.

I walked down the hallway, which smelled like bleach or some other kind of chemical. I entered room 303, and a very young and sour-looking teacher, Mr. King, I supposed, stopped talking and just stared at me. Every kid in the room looked up and stared as well.

"Name?" Mr. King finally barked.

"Blake Pendleton," I said. "I'm new." I was not going to add, *And I need training*. Screw that.

"Sir," he snapped back.

"No, just Blake," I responded. The class laughed.

"You address me as sir."

"Sorry. I'll try to remember that." *Oops.* "Sir," I added.

"Don't try, Pendleton. Do. Now sit." He nodded toward a desk at the back of the room. I quickly headed there and took my seat. I didn't remember school being such a hard-ass place. Once I sat down, I could see that all the other students had their phones in front of them on their desks. I set mine down in front of me as well.

There were words in large bold letters on the screen.

Follow the rules.

Do what is right.

Report rule breakers.

As I looked up, I could see the same words were on every student's phone. But all eyes were looking forward. Mr. King had just switched on an overhead projector. There was a video clip of a mass of people shouting and fighting in the street. Right. What was this class anyway? Supposedly it was political science.

"Nonconformity leads to chaos," Sir King said. "Chaos leads to conflict. Conflict leads to more chaos. More chaos leads to collapse. History shows us this pattern over and over."

And then something very weird happened. The entire class spoke at once, saying, "Until now." It made me jump. What was going on? When I looked down, there were the words on my phone. And on everyone else's phone. Those words. And everyone had automatically read them out loud at the same time.

"I couldn't hear you, Pendleton," the teacher barked. He'd been looking right at me and had seen that I hadn't joined in.

"Until now," I said in a stunned whisper.

"Louder."

Screw you, I wanted to shout. But I didn't. "Until now," I said, louder and with as much authority as I could muster. Which wasn't much.

King nodded and punched a remote that brought up a visual of a city street with people begging and trudging along, looking homeless and helpless. "Nonconformity, chaos, conflict, chaos, collapse. Economic disaster. An unbreakable cycle."

"Until now," the entire class replied.

I missed my cue again, but King didn't notice. His attention was on the video, which now showed a sunlit city street filled with smiling, happy people. He kept his back to the class.

Some guy three rows over waved at me, trying to get my attention. When I looked at him, he turned back toward the teacher, held a fist up in front of his face and defiantly raised his middle finger skyward. Then he quickly tucked it down under his desk just as King turned around to face the class.

The bell rang then, although it wasn't like any bell I remembered. It was a long, extremely loud burst of something that sounded like static. At once all the kids put their phones in their khaki shirt pockets and stood up. But they didn't move until Mr. King nodded. The guy who had done the one-finger salute looked my way again and shook his head slightly.

I sat there dumbfounded for a few seconds, taking a good look around the room for the first time. It felt like I was in some kind of bad dream. Mr. King was at his desk now, staring down at his own phone. It was only as I slowly got up to leave that I realized there wasn't a single book anywhere in the room.

Chapter Two

The guy from the class sidled up alongside me as soon as I was out of the room. "Walk," he said.

"But I don't know where I'm supposed to be next," I replied.

"It's on your phone, but we have five minutes. If you're cool, just walk with me for a bit. I know three dead zones in the school."

"Dead zones?"

"Places where they can't see or hear you."

"Who are they? And why are they watching and listening?"

"Just shut up and walk," he said. He never looked at me as he spoke. He kept his head down like he was staring at the floor.

I followed him to a hallway that looked like it was under construction. He grabbed my arm and led me past a plastic tarp stretched across the hall. There was no one on the other side.

"I'm Ming, by the way. And you're new here. Blake Pendleton, right?"

"Right."

"And clearly you are, like, from Mars or someplace. You don't know shit about the rules."

This guy was something else. "No, I'm not from Mars," I said. "But I sure feel like it. And you're right— I don't know shit about the rules."

"Don't tell anyone that."

"I just told you." What was with this guy?

"I won't report you. But others would. Here. You'll need this." Ming handed me a case for my phone. "It blocks the signal and makes it look like your freephone is temporarily not working."

"*Freephone?* Is it called that because they give them to you for free?"

"No, it's short for 'freedom phone.' It's what they call these little bastards."

"It's just a cell phone, right?"

"No. It's a tool they use to feed you what they want to feed you, to follow you and, if they want, to monitor your every move."

"They can't do that."

"They *do* do that. You really *are* out of touch, aren't you?"

"I've been away."

"Tell me about that."

"I don't know if I should. This whole scene is freaking me out. I don't understand what's going on. When we got back, I noticed a lot of changes, sure.

People acting kind of funny. Saying funny things. But I've only been back a week, and I'm still getting my land legs. I figured I just needed to adjust."

"No, man. Don't adjust. Don't. And what do you mean by 'land legs'? Where exactly have you been?"

Everything about the morning had thrown me off. I really didn't understand what had happened to the school—and maybe it was more than the school. I'd noticed people were acting formal, weird, kind of suspicious of my parents and me. Up until now I'd thought it was because we were different from being gone so long, and that we didn't fit in anymore.

I blinked, and I guess I looked kind of vacant. Ming seemed to read me like a book.

"Ah. You're not sure you should trust me. I understand. You're feeling suddenly paranoid. Paranoid is good. Hang on to that. So I will try to put you at ease. We only have a few minutes left, but I'll tell you a bit about me and then I'll get you to class."

He held out his hand for me to shake. I shook.

"Ming," he said, letting go. I knew that already. "Ming Zhao," he continued. "Please don't ask me where I'm from. Even though I was born and raised right here, people still ask. Yes, my grandparents were from China. My grandfather and grandmother were both athletes—very fast runners—and that brought them to North America. My father is an engineer. Or was an engineer. Mom is a psychologist and a good liar. That's why she still has a job. She pretends to be part of the New Order."

Again he read my blank look. I had no idea what the New Order was. Ming looked a little nervous now. "Shit. I have to get you to your next class." He grabbed my phone, took off the case and tapped the dark screen. "Room 416, English. Miss Carlyle. This way."

He led me to the stairway and pointed up. "Go. But meet me outside after school. I need to know your story." And then he was off, half running, half walking down the hall.

I hurried to find room 416 and shuffled to an empty desk, again at the back of the room. *Try to be invisible,* I told myself. *Try not to stand out.* I sat down and placed my phone on my desk in the same place as all the others students had. Words appeared on the screen now.

English only.

English is universal.

A single language. A single vision.

Simplify. Unify.

Defy foreigners.

The messages were prompts of some kind, I concluded, that related to the new rules and maybe this New Order thing. I remembered there had been a lot of talk about immigration and the economy before we'd left. People had been saying that immigrants were taking jobs away. That foreigners were dangerous. It hadn't made much sense to me.

The teacher walked into the room. She was young. Very young. Not much more than twenty-one,

I guessed. She looked the class over, noticed me but didn't say anything. I was happy about that. I scanned the room. The students were all facing forward. The walls had slogans on them I wasn't familiar with.

"Take out your dictionaries," Miss Carlyle said. But, as in the previous classroom, there were no books that I could see. Certainly not on the desks, which were just small tables without a storage space underneath. I noticed everyone picking up their phones. Fingers tapped in sync. I tried to tap as well, but all I got was a message.

Failed. Error. Correct immediately.

I stared at the device.

"Remember, students. You are only to use a word in accordance with definitions from this dictionary," the teacher said. "It has been carefully developed to keep the language consistent and pure. As I've said before, this is the only way communication can be clear. This way there is no misunderstanding.

Language abuse was part of the old system that your parents may remember. But that has been corrected."

The students nodded.

"Jason, will you read what your dictionary says under the word *freedom*?"

A ginger-haired kid near the front of the room read, " 'Freedom—the will to act in a way that is right, to act in accordance with accepted principles, to choose correctly without fail.' "

"Thank you, Jason," said Miss Carlyle.

Using her own phone, she flashed other words onto the whiteboard. Each was accompanied by an image. Then she asked for definitions, which various students read from their phones, one by one. All of them read in a monotone voice, and all read only what was on the screen. So this was English class. No discussion. No stories. No poetry. Just words and definitions.

"Creativity," said Miss Carlyle as the word and an image of a tall concrete building were projected onto the board. "How about you, new student? Identify yourself and speak."

Whoa. This was so weird. "Uh…I'm B-Blake," I stuttered. "Um, *creativity*…" My screen was now blank. I slowly, awkwardly, tried to key in the word, but I got nothing. Foolishly I decided to wing it. I shrugged. "Well, creativity. You know, using your imagination, um, being inventive. Thinking outside the box. Something like that."

There was a shocked silence in the room. Then somebody in the back of the room snickered.

The teacher shifted on her feet and frowned at me. "You weren't reading that from your screen, were you…Blake, was it?"

I shrugged again. "Sorry, I haven't quite got the hang of it yet."

"And what was that box you were referring to?"

"Sorry?"

"You said something about thinking outside the box. A very odd definition."

"It's just an expression."

"But we are working strictly on definitions here, not guesswork. Guesswork leads to error. And error leads to wrong thinking."

This was getting a bit ridiculous. "Look, I'm new, okay? I don't quite know the ropes."

She grimaced at my choice of words again. "The *rules*, you mean?"

Jeez, lady. "Yes, I suppose so. The rules." I should have stopped talking right there. Kept my mouth shut. Apologized, even though I hadn't done anything wrong. But now I was getting pissed off. "Who came up with these rules anyway?" I asked. The words just sort of jumped out.

I could tell by the sound of other kids sucking in their breath and then the hush that fell over the room that this most definitely had been the wrong thing to say.

The teacher walked to her desk, tapped her phone once and spoke into it. "Mr. Tulane, I'm sending down a student for Level One." She looked at a boy sitting close to the door and said, "Gregory, will you escort this young man down to Mr. Tulane?"

Gregory nodded and stood up immediately. I received an icy stare from Miss Definition Cop as I grudgingly got up and followed Gregory out of the room. In truth, I was somewhat relieved to be leaving.

"You really pissed off Miss Carlyle," said Gregory when we were a few steps down the hall. But when he saw me open my mouth to reply, he put his finger to his lips and pointed up to the right and left. Cameras. Equipped, I assumed, with microphones.

Mr. Tulane turned out to be the pinch-faced man who had greeted me that morning and given me the phone. "Level One, is it," he said to me. More of a statement than a question.

I felt like a little kid again, a little kid who had just peed his pants. I decided to keep my mouth shut this time.

"This way."

Gregory faded back into the hallway as I followed Mr. Tulane past a series of offices to an open door that led into a bare, windowless room. "Level One it is," he said. "Welcome." He gestured for me to step inside. Then he closed the door. I heard the lock click.

I was alone. Very alone. A harsh light shone down from the ceiling. No windows, no furniture. But, strangely, I still had my phone. Or *their* phone. Very weird. I took it out of my pocket, sucked in a deep breath and tried to figure out what the hell was going on.

Then the phone buzzed once with the same sound that had signaled the end of class. It lit up.

Level One

Three hours' isolation.

I stared at the screen, then typed in a question.

Why am I here?

An answer appeared immediately. No doubt an automatic response.

Inappropriate behavior. Level One is for correction.

And then the screen went dark. I tried to turn it back on but got nothing.

I leaned against the shiny concrete wall and decided to simply play it cool. Lesson of the day, I figured, was try to fit in, don't ask questions, and don't rock the boat. Just go by the book. But I didn't know what the book was.

I felt like smashing that stupid phone. But I didn't.

I wondered if I would ever learn what had happened to the school in the time I'd been away. Something bizarre. Some kind of backlash—but a backlash against what?

I stood up and yanked on the door handle. Still locked. I wanted to kick it, but I calmed myself down and went back to leaning against the bare wall. I remembered what my father had taught me about panic and fear and doing irrational things in desperate situations.

Stay calm, Blake. Use your head. Assess the situation and then decide what to do. And remember, if you don't fully understand what's going on, if you can't decide what to do, sometimes it's better to do nothing at all.

So I slid down the wall until I was sitting on the floor. I closed my eyes and visualized being back on the *Blue Dolphin* on a quiet, sunny morning before my parents were awake. I had the sea all to myself. And it was beautiful and calm.

Chapter Three

Three hours is a long time when you are alone with no way of tracking the time. The phone stayed dead. After a while I felt another wave of panic, so I concentrated on conjuring the voice of my father again to calm me. He, my mother and the sea had taught me a lot in the three years we'd been away. How I wished we were still out there on the boat, sailing from island to island, seemingly a million miles from North America.

Finally I heard the door lock click. I stood up and tried the handle. It opened. My knees were stiff as I began to move. I went out and made my way down the hallway, looking into the offices lining the corridor as I walked. Each office was empty. I continued walking, still not seeing anyone. Where was the way out of this damn school anyway? I heard some kind of cheering coming from way down the hall and headed toward it. Just then an old man in a drab gray uniform popped out from one of the offices. He had a mop and a bucket. The janitor, I figured.

"Aren't you supposed to be in assembly?" he asked.

"I don't know, am I?"

He looked at me suspiciously. But then his face softened.

"Ah, new boy. Let me guess. First Level One?"

"Last Level One," I replied.

He laughed. And I realized it was the first time I had heard anyone laugh since arriving at this hellhole they called a school. I studied his face.

"Rodriguez," he said. "I've been here quite a while. I've seen a lot of changes these last few years."

"I've noticed," I said.

"Got a name?"

"Blake."

"Blake, you ain't gonna like it here, but you'll need to adjust."

"I know. The rules, right?"

He laughed again. "People always coming up with new ways to make you do things you don't want to do. But you didn't hear that from me."

I nodded down the hall toward where the noise was coming from. Assembly. "What am I supposed to do now?"

"Well, everyone else is in assembly. It's kind of like an old pep rally. Only worse. I wouldn't walk in there right now. People get all worked up and then like to draw attention to anyone who's different. Someone'll see you right away, and you'll be in trouble."

"But I was locked in a damn room. What was I supposed to do?"

"I know. But it doesn't matter. Now you're late for assembly."

"What happens if I just walk out the front door and go home?"

"That's trouble too. Probably bigger trouble."

"Then what am I supposed to do?"

Rodriguez just shrugged and clapped me on the shoulder. "Damned if you do, damned if you don't. Sorry, Blake."

What the hell? I thanked him, turned and then walked out the front door. It was a cloudy, cold and windy day that made me miss the warmer weather of the southern seas. The wind blowing through me was bitter, but it felt good to be out of the school and on my own.

I didn't even think about where I was going. I just started walking. Right away my damn phone started buzzing again. I figured it had detected that I'd gone AWOL. That's when I heard someone shouting from behind me. Shouting my name. *Hell.* What now?

My instinct was to start running, but then I heard a second person shouting—a girl. I stopped. I turned.

Two students were running my way. One of them was Ming. The girl didn't look familiar. They both were running like they were in a race, like star athletes. Ming was having trouble keeping up. I stopped and waited until they reached me. All the while, my damn phone kept buzzing.

Both of them were breathing heavily when they caught up to me, and as soon as he was close enough, Ming punched me in the chest.

Or I thought he punched me in the chest. He was actually grabbing my phone from my pocket. He took it from me without speaking and slipped that heavy case over it. He handed it back.

"Rule number one. When you leave school, shield your freaking phone."

"No more rules," I said.

"Well," Ming said, catching his breath, "there are rules and there are *rules*. C'mon, keep walking."

We walked. As soon as we began to move, the girl grabbed my hand. "I'm Gina. Ming told me all about you. How was Level One?"

"How do you know about that?"

"A lucky guess. Most new students screw up the first day and end up in isolation. Just the way it goes."

"I thought punishment like that went out with the Dark Ages."

"Welcome to the new Dark Ages," Ming said. "Do you hate it or do you hate it?"

"I think I hate it. But I don't understand why all this is happening. I don't understand why you guys put up with this shit."

"Not everyone does," Gina said. "*We* don't. Or, at least, we try not to let it get to us."

Ming tried to shush her. "Watch what you are

saying, Gina. We don't really even know this nerdy guy yet. He could be one of Tulane's spies."

"Does he look like a spy?" Gina asked.

Ming grabbed my arm and stopped me. He looked right into my eyes. "Now that you mention it, he looks like a very confused and unhappy boy. He's got that deer-caught-in-the-headlights look." He chuckled. "But maybe Level One didn't exactly drain his brain like they'd hoped."

I tried to explain how both my father and my mother had trained me for difficult situations.

"Wait a minute," Gina said. "So you're saying you were on a boat for three years? That explains a lot."

We had stopped in a park. And I suddenly noticed we were surrounded by trees—tall hemlock trees that looked green and healthy. One of the first things I'd noticed when we returned was how few trees were left in town. I'd seen plenty of stumps by the sidewalks, but most of the trees were gone.

"It was their dream," I continued. "They're both sailors. We've owned a sailboat ever since I can remember. Went out to sea for weekends, sometimes longer. My father would play with his little drone camera and take pictures of us from up in the sky. Then they both quit their jobs—said they didn't like the direction everything was going in."

"'Everything' meaning politics, government and popular opinion about what is and isn't important?" Ming asked.

"You took the words out of my mouth. So that was three years ago. They sold everything, including our house, and we just—"

"Sailed away," Gina said, completing my sentence. She had a wistful look in her eyes. "But you must have known how things were changing. They must have known."

"Maybe. But I was just a kid. I wasn't really paying attention. My parents made a point of not listening to the news. All I knew was that I missed home. Missed my friends, video games, Netflix. Even school. Everything. But after a while I grew to love it. The sea. Life on the *Blue Dolphin*. Sailing from island to island in the South Pacific. I mean, my parents drove me nuts plenty of times with their preachy stuff about being environmentally responsible and not sucking up planetary resources. But they were right. And eventually I got into the groove."

"It sounds amazing," Gina said. "Like a dream come true."

"Why did you come back?" Ming asked.

I threw up my hands. "I'm not quite sure. There was this feeling that came over all three of us at around the same time. We missed…well, we missed home. Only problem was, when we got here, home didn't feel like home anymore. How could so much change in three years?"

"I'm not sure anyone can answer that," Gina told me. "I mean, I can hardly remember what things were like before the New Order. People were already losing their jobs to new technology. Then the pandemic caught everyone off guard. The economy dipped. People lost jobs, houses. Technology put a lot of skilled workers out of work. Leaders wanted to blame someone, so they targeted intellectuals, liberals and especially immigrants."

"I get dirty looks every bloody day," Ming said. "Nobody cares that I was born here. They just assume I don't belong."

"Yeah, and my family gets treated like second-class citizens because we're Black," said Gina.

"But I still don't get it," I said. "How did everyone let schools turn into—?"

"Brainwashing prisons?" Gina finished for me. "Brainwashing prisons that parents voluntarily send their kids to?"

"Not exactly what I was going to say, but okay, that."

"Well, not everybody but a big chunk of the population became convinced that thinking for yourself, independent thinking, leads to chaos, and chaos leads to disorder, and what we needed was more order, more discipline, more following the rules."

"But who makes up these fucking rules?" The words came out louder and more forcefully than I'd intended.

"*They* do," Ming outright shouted. "The great invisible *they*. And now everyone else does what *they* tell them to do."

"Everyone but us," Gina said.

Chapter Four

My head hurt from thinking about school and listening to Ming and Gina. I needed to go home. I said goodbye to them, and Ming said, "Keep the phone case. You can't leave it on all the time, though, or they'll know. So take the case off, and when you get home put the phone in your closet or your sock drawer. Our idiot classmates think it's cool that the school gives you a freephone. But you pay a price. They use it to track you and listen in. You can put on the shield once in a while and they think it's just a temporary glitch, but at school you have to leave your phone on pretty much all the time."

"And don't tell them where you got the case," Gina added.

"Where *did* you get it?" I asked.

"I made it," Ming said. "But you must never tell anyone, even someone you think you trust."

Their insistence on secrecy made me wonder why they trusted me. As I walked away, I thought about what kind of trouble I might get in if I didn't play by the new rules. Was there a Level Two punishment? A Level Three? That only made my head hurt more.

When I got home, my parents looked as glum as I did. I kept my "freephone" and the case in my pocket and sat down at the kitchen table. My mom was sipping her herbal tea, and my father was peeling the label off a half-empty bottle of beer.

"How was school?" my mom asked.

"Unreal," I answered.

"What do you mean?" Dad asked, frowning. And my father rarely frowns.

"I'll explain later." I really didn't want to talk about it. "What's up with you two?" I hadn't seen them look this defeated since our mast snapped in two halfway between Fiji and Australia.

"We both went looking for work," my mom said, dipping the tea bag in and out of her cup. "But we didn't have much luck."

"No one wants to take us on because we've been out of the country for more than two years. Apparently we need to apply to have our citizenship renewed before we can even begin to look for work. Can you believe it?"

"But we were all born here! We grew up here." This day was getting crazier by the minute.

"I know, son. But that doesn't seem to matter anymore," my dad said, still focused on removing the paper label from the bottle. "We're considered immigrants now. We need to apply as if we have never lived here before. And there's some courses we have to take too."

"New rules," my mom added. "Something like that."

My dad sucked in his breath. "I'm thinking that maybe we should just haul up the anchor and head back to sea. How would you feel about that?"

"I'm in," I said. After my disastrous first day of school, I loved the thought of getting the hell away.

"I don't know," my mom said. "Maybe we just need a bit more time to adjust. I'm not sure running away is the answer."

"Sailing away," my father corrected.

Already, like him, I found myself missing our days traveling at sea and visiting foreign places. It hadn't always been easy like in some fantasy movie, but it had always been interesting. We'd even weathered the broken mast. The three of us had managed to fashion a makeshift sail that got us into port safely. "See, Blake?" my dad had said. "Anything can be fixed. All problems have solutions."

But looking at the worried faces of my parents now, I could see they weren't feeling so optimistic about this new situation.

On day two at school, I pretty much kept to myself. I left the so-called freephone on and spoke to others as little as I could. I didn't see Gina and Ming anywhere, but it was a big school. I kept studying the faces of the other students in class. Most seemed strangely attentive. But then, many of them could have been faking it. After all, there were cameras everywhere, and the phones let someone or some program track their every move. I went to my math, history and biology classes and couldn't help noticing how young most of the teachers were. Really young, like twenty or maybe twenty-one. Tulane was an old guy, but I wondered how the others could even be teachers yet. What they all had in common was a rigid style.

No students could ask questions. There were no real discussions. A teacher would say something, and kids would look at their phones. The teacher would call on someone, and they would answer with what they saw on the screen. There were only right answers. All provided by that damn little screen. History class was the worst. It didn't make any sense. I had read plenty of history books while I was on the boat. About World War I. World War II. Afghanistan. Iraq. None of them were even mentioned in class.

Miss Jamieson, the history teacher, was a bit of a puzzle to me. Like the others, she was young. She didn't look like someone who would just follow orders. But she acted exactly like all the other teachers. I wondered if she was faking it. And I wondered again how many other kids were faking it.

I wanted to ask Ming or Gina if they thought Miss Jamieson might be different, but when I finally spotted them in the hall, they both ignored me. It was like we'd never had that conversation in the park. *What the hell?*

Somehow I got through the day. And the next. And the one after that. And all I learned was that it was best to keep quiet. Answer from the phone if called upon. Write the answers they wanted on their stupid tests, and, above all, lie low and not draw attention to myself.

And then one day Gina walked past me in the hall and stuffed a note into my pocket. We were in the middle of a crowd of kids rushing to class. When the coast was clear, I pulled it out.

Sorry for the cold shoulder. M and I are under watch.

Will talk when we can. Hang in there.

So I hung in. What I was waiting for, I had no idea.

A week went by and then two. Things were pretty bad at home. My parents had both reapplied for citizenship. They had been told I didn't have to as long as I was in school. After attending several mandatory "citizen renewal" sessions, they were getting more and more discouraged.

I'd adopted a kind of zombielike presence at school that worked amazingly well. But after a while, I really was starting to feel a bit undead. I'd seen a couple of kids get into trouble in class and sent off to Tulane. One of them, an edgy, nervous kid named Jordan, begged Mr. King not to send him to the office. He said something about not being able to handle Level Two, but Mr. King didn't budge. I wasn't sure I could handle Level Two either, even though I had no idea what it was. I desperately wanted to talk to Ming and Gina, the only two kids in school who had reached out to me in the whole month I'd been there. But they continued to pretend they didn't know me, and I didn't want to push it.

Actually, a couple of thugs had reached out to me, but not in a good way. Curtis and Gleeson were big, hulking twelfth graders who had singled me out more than once to give me a hard time. It usually happened in the bathroom. The fact that they'd started harassing me while I was trying to take a pee almost seemed normal. The first time, Gleeson did most of the talking.

"New kid, right?"

"Right."

"Think you're smart, don't you?"

"Not necessarily."

"What the fuck is that supposed to mean?"

"Doesn't mean anything other than that." I finished my business and turned around, zipping up.

"Some of us don't like it when we work hard to get through school and some asshole like you just shows up and thinks he can slip on through."

"I appreciate that," I said in my most diplomatic voice.

Gleeson turned to Curtis. "Did you hear that? He says he *appreciates* that."

Gleeson turned to walk away. I thought that was that, but he suddenly shuffled backward and, still with his back to me, slammed an elbow into my groin. I doubled over in pain as the two of them walked out of the bathroom, slamming the door against the wall. Then that damn buzzer sounded. Time for class.

Chapter Five

I guess it was inevitable. I had to stumble again sometime. It happened in math class. An overly loud teacher named Mr. Mallick yammered away daily about numbers and equations and the importance of all manner of things being what he called "numerically correct." And on this day I just couldn't focus on the quadratic equation on the whiteboard. My eyes refused to stay open.

I wasn't the first to fall asleep in his class, I'm sure. And in the old days, a pissed-off math teacher would have walked up to a snoring kid like me and slammed a big textbook down on the desk. But now there were no books, remember? So I was blasted awake by a deafening screech ripping through my brain. Mr. Mallick was holding his freephone up to my ear.

The other kids loved the drama. I had no idea what was going on.

"Level Two, Pendleton. Now."

So Level Two it was. No one had explained to me yet what it meant, but I was about to find out.

Tulane's assistant, a guy maybe only a year or two older than me with close-cropped hair and a shiny face, led me out. He was wearing the usual khaki uniform, but his had two blue stripes on the sleeve. We stopped in front of a room farther down the dark hall from the first one I'd been in.

"You going to tell me what happens in Level Two?" I asked.

"Nothing," he said smugly. "Nothing at all."

Oh, right. So it was more of the isolation for me. "How long?"

"You'll find out," he said, opening the metal door. "Phone." He held out his hand.

Somewhat surprised, I gave him my phone. At least it meant they couldn't feed me their bullshit propaganda messages while I was in there.

I'm not really sure why I didn't just run right then. I guess it was because I knew these isolation punishments were meant to break me in some way, and part of me wanted to prove I couldn't be broken.

But as the door closed with a loud thud, I suddenly felt scared and completely cut off from the outside world. Now I was confined to a room in a building more like a prison than a place of learning.

Bare gray walls and ceiling. No windows. Gray concrete floor. A bank of all-too-bright overhead fluorescent lights. And some kind of hum. Fairly loud. Ventilation system, I figured at first, but as

I stood there listening to it, I thought there was something a bit odd about it. Was I hearing voices? Dull, hushed voices? Maybe, maybe not.

I assumed there was some kind of hidden camera up in the lights. I was sure I was being watched. Everyone was watched at this school. The minutes ticked by. I had no way of knowing how much time had passed or how long I'd have to remain here.

Be cool. Don't break. Go deep inside. Stay there. Visualize.

I had lots of calming images to choose from. The sea on a warm, dark night. The waves glowing with bioluminescent plankton. The moon high in the sky, its reflection glinting off the calm water. The dawn. The sea breeze smelling like salt. The wind filling the sail. More images filled my head. The drone footage my father loved to take in the mornings. My mother, father and me looking up into the sky from the deck of *Blue Dolphin*. We'd watched that footage a dozen times since returning to land. It was like an impossible fantasy of some sort. It had been real. Once. I had to remember that. But how long could I stay inside my mind and rely on memories to keep me from going mad? I guessed I was going to find that out as well.

After I got the first wave of panic under control, I lay down on the cold concrete floor and tried to sleep. Napping had always been a skill of mine, one I'd picked up from my father. "A twenty-minute nap in the middle of the day, and I'm good to go another ten hours," he'd say, prepping himself for a night watch at the helm. He'd trained me to do it—the nap and then the night watch. I'd never felt more alive than being the only one awake at 3 a.m., keeping watch in the middle of the ocean.

Everything about life ashore, back in our former world, was the opposite of those calming memories. I couldn't nap. There was something about the humming sound. It had grown louder while I had been in here. And those voices I thought I heard. I couldn't make out the words, but they were definitely there. I started to feel detached from myself.

You start to go crazy after a while—and there is no way of telling how long "a while" is. And you go more crazy. Then you regroup and muster your courage, your focus. You fight the dark thoughts. Then you go even more crazy. Bang on the door. Yell. Scream. Admit defeat and beg to be let out.

And then you give up. You hold your hands over your ears to keep out the hum and the voices that whisper nonstop. You sit down in a corner. You huddle. You fall over on your side and curl up into a fetal position. You go crazy some more, wondering when it will end. When you'll be allowed to go back into the world.

And then it gets worse. Has it been an hour? Two? Who knows? You know you're being watched, so you speak out, admit defeat. You promise to follow instructions, to not ask questions, to fall into line, to be good.

You do all that. And nothing happens. You feel a new wave of panic and hopelessness shoot through your body. And still it goes on.

And then it's over.

Tulane himself opened the door. He was smiling. "Get up, Pendleton. Time to go home." He handed me my phone. "Remember, keep it with you, and keep it on at all times. Waking or sleeping."

I heard myself say meekly, "Yes, sir. Thank you."

The school day had been over for a while. When I looked at my screen, I saw I'd been in Level Two punishment for six hours. My thoughts were all foggy. *Did I fall asleep? Or was I in some kind of half-sleeping dream state, some kind of semi-conscious nightmare? Did I really stay in there for six hours? Did it even happen?* Regardless, I knew I couldn't ever go through that again. Never. I needed to pay better attention to the rules.

The schoolyard was empty when I left the building, and it was getting dark. My parents would be worried. I started walking home. Everything looked alien and unfamiliar. As I turned down a side street, I heard a voice from a basement doorway.

"Blake, over here. Stop."

I looked but didn't see anyone in the gloom.

"The case I gave you," the voice said. "Put it back on your phone." It was Ming.

I looked at my phone, then fished in my pants pocket for the case and slipped it on. Ming walked up the steps and stood in front of me. "They let you go. Right on time. Level Two. Six hours. How'd you do?"

My head was still full of fog and noise. And voices. "I don't know. It was bloody awful."

"Some kids crack. Some of the best of them roll right over. It's amazing how little it takes to turn a good, freethinking human being into an obedient machine."

"Is that what they're trying to do?"

"Yeah. C'mon. Follow me to Gina's. We have something we need to share with you."

"I need to go home. I feel awful. And my parents will be freaking."

"Let them freak. We need to talk."

Chapter Six

"Come right in. Gina's upstairs," Gina's mom said when she opened the door of their apartment. I followed Ming up to Gina's bedroom. She was sitting at a desk, reading a book. Flashy posters covered the walls—Malcolm X, Jimi Hendrix, Che Guevara, Nelson Mandela. Clearly Gina admired those who challenged the system. But it was the book that drew my attention.

Gina noticed my stare and smiled. "Nothing will ever replace the smell and feel of a real book," she said. "How did Level Two go?"

I was still feeling too stunned to even answer.

Ming answered for me. "He made it through. His head hurts, but he's here with us."

"Is it time?" Gina asked.

"Definitely," Ming said.

"Can we trust him?"

"It's now or never," Ming said, punching me good-naturedly on the shoulder.

"We've both done Level Three," Gina said. "Ming's dad coached both of us on how to handle it. Nine hours."

"*Nine hours?*" I said. "Isn't there some kind of law against that? It's torture!"

"That *is* the law," Ming said. "My father had it worse. Special courses for anyone of Chinese descent. But his father, my grandfather, went through similar so-called training before moving here. He passed down the skills he learned about controlling your thoughts."

"And emotions," Gina added. "Ming's dad got through it. But my dad is still in reconditioning. He asked too many questions. He's been away for three months."

"Prison?"

"Not exactly. He didn't break any real law. At his job, they just told him he wasn't fitting in. He wasn't following instructions the way they wanted him to. So he was nominated for recon."

"*Nominated* is a nice way of saying he had to go or he would lose his job," Ming added. "My father is highly skilled at sliding through the system, saying what they want him to say, acting the way they want him to act. All the while maintaining his dignity. Inside."

"My parents are having a hard time fitting back in," I admitted. "I'm worried about them."

"You should be," Gina said. "But first let's talk about us. Let's talk about you. What did you hear when you were in Level Two?"

"I thought I heard voices, but maybe it was just the ventilation fan."

"No. You definitely heard voices. Very soft. But very real. They were subliminal messages. Stupid stuff. *Do what's right. Follow instructions. Trust authority. Rule breakers will be punished.*"

"I don't think I heard any of that."

"Yes, you did," Gina said. "It's a program. We've all been studying exactly how it works."

"We?" I asked.

"Dogs," Ming said. "We call ourselves Dogs. Underdogs. Superdogs. But dogs. It was my father who came up with it. Long ago there used to be signs in stores and restaurants right here in town. *No Chinamen or dogs.*"

Gina added, "Same sort of thing for Black people."

"Dogs hear what their masters don't. Often they see what their masters don't. That's us. We are watching and listening. And we are not alone."

"You have some kind of organization?"

"A loose network. Can't really be too organized, or we'll get shut down. But Gina and I have had our own training. My dad helped, like I said. So did her mom. Her father too, until he was lifted out of his job. And you're going to have to watch out for your parents."

"How can I do that? I can barely watch out for myself."

"No choice, brother. Be strong. There's a lot to lose."

"Looks like it's already lost."

Ming laughed. "I agree, it does seem that way, but there's hope. There's always been an underground."

The word rang a few bells from things I'd read before I left school and later, on the boat. "And dogs dig underground?"

"Something like that. Are you in?"

"Yeah, I'm in."

"Then you have to start playing by the rules. Their rules. In fact, you need to convince Tulane and his grunts that you want to be one of them. Convince them that Level Two was enough. Notice how young a lot of the teachers and administrators are?"

"Yeah, I did think it was kind of odd."

"They like young. Means they're easier to mold. So if you can convince Tulane you want a career as a teacher or a cop or a lawyer or even a politician, they'll fast-track you. You'll get what they call induction training. It's a fancy word for what's basically brainwashing. It's pretty intense."

"Why not just keep my head down and pretend and just get through the bullshit and finish school?"

Gina looked at me doubtfully. "There is no finishing school. You might get through twelfth grade and not return to the building, but the training continues. Mandatory meetings. Digital daily programs. It never ends. The only hope is to get enough of us into positions of authority."

"Dogs on top."

"Right."

"Sounds impossible."

"It probably is," Ming said. "But Gina and I volunteered for induction. And we got past the first phase. Twenty-four hours of isolation. No light and no sound except for the noise you heard. With the voices. Only they don't call it punishment. They call it training."

so many others, I'd thought stuff like that couldn't happen here. But apparently it could.

And I hated what had happened to my home.

Still, I wasn't entirely sure I wanted to be one of Ming and Gina's so-called Dogs. From what I'd seen of school, the system was set. The rules were hard and fast. And I wasn't sure anything was going to change it back to the way it had been. I especially wasn't sure I had the nerve or the ability to help make the change. Maybe Gina and Ming and all those others were just kidding themselves. They'd get caught, and they'd get punished. God only knew how many punishment levels there were. Better to just think of the alternative. Convince my parents we'd made a bad decision coming home. We still had a boat moored in the harbor. All we had to do was pack up, motor out to sea and sail away.

Those days on deck in the south came back to haunt me again on this cold, dark day with another nasty wind blowing dust and litter down the street.

Days on deck with a soft sea breeze, me lying there reading a book.

My parents had used the money from selling our nice little house for the trip. I missed the old place sometimes. I missed my old bedroom. I missed my posters on the wall. Posters of tropical islands, crystal-clear lagoons, a nighttime sea lit up with plankton. On our travels, those images from my walls had become the images of my everyday life. How lucky was that? But then we had decided to come back.

Now I was walking up the stairs to our crappy second-floor apartment in a rundown brick building, dreaming of nothing but escape. I opened the door and walked in.

My father was bent over at the kitchen table, holding his head in his hands. My mom had her hand on his shoulder. When they heard me come in, he looked up, and I could see he'd been crying.

"Your father's had a rough day," my mom said.

She was the rock of our family. My dad was pretty tough too. But he showed his emotions more than she did. Once he'd had a good cry, he'd bounce right back. Give a little speech and start working on a solution. But this seemed bigger.

"What happened?" I asked.

"Harbor patrol impounded our boat," my dad said, blowing his nose and pulling himself back together.

"Why?" I asked.

"They say it's because of taxes," Mom said. "We didn't file our income tax forms while we were gone."

"But we didn't have any income," I said.

"No, but that doesn't seem to matter," my father said. "And it's my fault. When I applied for a job last week, the interviewer asked me about my job and income from the past three years, and I told him the truth. So he must have accessed my tax records. And then he turned me in."

"But you didn't do anything wrong."

"Doesn't matter. They've confiscated the boat. It's still there in the water, but I have a court order saying we can't touch it."

So much for my daydream of us hopping back on and sailing the hell out of here.

"We may have to pay some kind of fine," my mother said. "And if we can't pay, there's a possibility that one or both of us will have to go to jail."

"That's insane."

"Everything here is insane," my father said, pounding the table with his fist.

"And because we're being charged with what they call tax fraud, no one is willing to hire us," added my mom.

"No job. No money," my dad said, looking more angry now than sad. "No way to even hire a lawyer. No way out."

"What can I do to help?" I asked. It all sounded so hopeless.

"Nothing," my mom said. "We don't belong here anymore. But now we can't leave. You need to be very careful, Blake. Stay out of trouble. Follow the rules."

There was that damned word again.

I should have sat down at the table with them and tried to console them somehow, but I was feeling a rising tide of rage inside me. I turned and marched off to my room.

I sat down on my bed and stared at the plain walls. I set my phone down on the small metal desk and took it out of the case shield, remembering what Ming had said. I could leave it in the shield for up to an hour at a time before anyone might think it wasn't just a technical glitch, but after that an algorithm might detect something suspicious. And I didn't want that.

As soon as I took the case off, the screen lit up. A message from school.

Induction rally Tuesday. All students invited. Free pizza.

I realized then that Ming and Gina were right. If you can't fight them, join them. But do it on your own terms. Do it to get on the inside.

Chapter Eight

The induction rally was like the old pep rallies we used to have in junior high. It was led by a recent graduate named Benjamin, who acted like he was a rock star. He used buzzwords and phrases like "self-improvement," "doing the right thing" and "understanding the big picture." He made induction sound like the most exciting thing a person could do in life. Every time he spouted one of those one-liners phrases—"brave new world order," "enlightenment," "solidarity," "the future is yours." And I kept thinking, No, the future isn't ours. Words could have the very opposite meaning of the truth. In fact, Benjamin Dinglehead even used the word *truth* fairly often and borrowed lines I'd seen in books years earlier. "The truth will set you free!" he shouted as the crowd roared again. Yeah, I kept thinking, but whose truth is that?

About halfway into his sermon, Benjamin paused briefly to describe how the induction worked. "Once you get accepted—and only the best and brightest of you will succeed—you will finish your eleventh year in pre-induction, and then you will complete your final year in school in full induction mode. Those of you who get through can come back to teach here the following year. You leap from student to teacher in one year. Or you can take an important job outside the school—in law enforcement, government work, immigration control. Whatever it is, you will be seen by everyone as a leader in the community." Then he stopped and took a deep breath. A hush fell over the crowd. His timing was clearly deliberate. Just before the crowd started to get restless, he spoke again. "How many of you in eleventh grade are ready to apply?"

Hands shot up around me. Mine too. I looked around and spotted Ming. He was standing up and waving. Gina was somewhere here too, I was sure, but I couldn't see her. I followed Ming's lead. I stood up and waved my hands over my head.

This training explained why the teachers were all so young. And why they seemed so keen to uphold the system. Induction was clearly intense training—a deep dive into all the rules and how to enforce them. I wondered if Ming and Gina were right. Could we really put ourselves through it and then use our positions of privilege to change the system? I had my doubts, but I didn't see a better alternative. Still, what if we were found out? What if our motives were revealed somehow? I didn't want to think about what the punishment would be.

My mom finally convinced the labor board to allow her to work part-time in a government office. It was a boring office job she was overqualified for, but we needed the money. My father was turned down for work again and again—always related to his having been out of the country for so long and the back-taxes issue. He attended courses that were supposed to bring him up to speed on the changes in the workplace and the community. He said he hated every minute of them. We just weren't the same happy family anymore. An air of desperation hung over the dinner table at night. My dad especially seemed beaten down, defeated.

Ming coached me for the polygraph test. Controlled breathing. Visualization. Distraction and relaxation techniques. He even taught me how to slow my heart rate. He was a most excellent teacher.

Three weeks went by. If all went well, I'd soon be out of regular classes and streamed into induction. But first there was the polygraph. It was making me nervous. And nervous is exactly what you don't want when taking that test. I understood what Ming had told me about eye movement, muscle tension, mental relaxation techniques, but I didn't know if I could do those things. I wasn't sure anyone could.

When I confessed this to Gina, she looked worried. But we were in the hall, with camera eyes on us and microphones in the walls. She just smiled and walked away, but later that day she walked up to me, took my hand and held it up to her face. This didn't seem like her at all. She looked deep into my eyes, closed my hand into a fist and quickly walked away.

She had left a slip of paper in my hand, but I didn't open my fist until I was pretty sure no one was watching.

Meet me in the park by the big hemlock tree after school.

Very important.

So I did. And Gina wasn't alone.

She had a teacher with her. Miss Jamieson, the history teacher. *What the bloody hell?* Was this some kind of a trap?

They were both sitting on a bench, watching me approach. Once again I was struck by how young Miss J. was.

I stood there in front of the two of them and said nothing.

"Blake," Gina said. "Miss Jamieson is going to give you a few more tips on how to pass the lie detector test."

I looked at this teacher, trying to figure out her intentions. But her face revealed nothing.

"Why?" I asked.

"Because I passed it myself," said Miss Jamieson.

"So?"

"So I was lying."

"And why are you telling me this?"

"Because she's one of us," Gina said.

"I don't understand," I said. "She's a teacher. She upholds the rules."

"I do," Jamieson agreed, "because I do what I have to do to stay in the school."

"Not all teachers like the way things are now," Gina added. "Some of them who went through induction held on to their belief that the new system is wrong and needs to go. Miss Jamieson is one of them. She's here to help us. To help you."

My gut told me no. She wasn't to be trusted. I knew the way she had corrected me in class. I'd listened to her version of history in the classroom. A version that didn't match at all what I'd read in books. Wasn't she one of *them*?

"Blake," Miss Jamieson said. "I was in school when things began to shift toward the new rules system. I watched as so much was changing in our lives. I wanted to fight it. But I saw what happened to people who did. Some lost their jobs. Some finished school and never got a job. Some ended up on the street or even went into hiding. I didn't want any of that to happen to me. So I went through induction. But I didn't let it change who I really am. And when I learned about the underground—the Dogs—I offered to help out in any way I can. That's why I'm here. I can help you pass the polygraph, but after that it's up to you."

Gina nodded. It was all some kind of crazy game, right? Or was it the real thing? If I couldn't trust Gina and Ming, then I couldn't trust anyone. "Okay," I said. "What do I have to do?"

"You need to relax," she said.

Obviously. So I tried hard to relax. I took deep breaths. I closed my eyes as instructed and let Jamieson guide me through some mental exercises that I guess you could say were part meditation, part distraction, part self-hypnosis. When she succeeded in getting me to a deep state of relaxation, she asked me about my "happy place."

Suddenly I was back on the deck of the boat. And everything in the world was okay. Somehow I knew that if I could follow this technique and ultimately take my mind to that place, I could pass any physical or psychological aspects of the polygraph test that might try to trip me up. *Let's do this.*

Chapter Nine

The following Monday I arrived at school early and walked straight into the office. I asked if I could meet with Mr. Tulane. The woman behind the counter remembered me and eyed me suspiciously. "In trouble again, Mr. Pendleton?"

"No," I said. "Nothing like that."

She was still looking at me like I'd just stolen money from her purse. "I'll see if he is available."

She picked up the phone and a few seconds later looked up. "He says you can go right in."

Mr. Tulane's door was open. He was looking intently at his computer as he motioned for me to sit down in the chair in front of his desk. I sat and waited. He was listening to some kind of speech. I could make out several phrases, but that was all—"new wave of unwanted," "repatriation issues," "formal preparation," "unacceptable backlash." The words didn't mean much to me, but it sounded a lot like the messages flashing on our phones and the stuff teachers said in class.

When the speech ended, Tulane nodded at the screen and clasped his hands together. There was a look of satisfaction on his face. He made one last click on his keyboard and then looked at me. He scowled.

"Pendleton, right?"

"Yes, sir."

"And why are you here?"

"To volunteer for induction training."

"You liked what you heard at the rally?"

"I did. I believe I'm up for the challenge."

He looked skeptical. Who could blame him?

"One day a troublemaker, and the next you want to be considered for privilege?"

"Yes, I know it seems odd. But that time in isolation gave me lots of time to think. I know I want to do something worthwhile with my life."

"And that would be what?"

"Get the proper training and become a teacher."

"Not everyone is cut out for that."

"I understand. But I believe I am."

"To be honest, I highly doubt you'll be able to pass the testing."

"Would you give me the chance to try? I won't let you down."

Tulane studied me rather intently now. His pale blue eyes seemed to burn holes right through my head. I had to hold his gaze and not look away. Could he tell what I was really thinking?

Finally he spoke. "Try, you said. And when would you like to try?"

"As soon as possible," I said. *Why wait around? Just do it.*

"Today, then. First battery of tests. You sure you're prepared for this?"

"Yes, sir," I said. "I am sure."

A pause, an extended awkward moment in which I could have cracked and said I was only joking, that I hated him and the whole bloody school, which was an educational nightmare.

He suddenly smiled and stood up. "Then let's begin. Follow me."

I followed him down that long hall I had walked before. But it wasn't to an isolation room this time. I entered another windowless room with about thirty cubicles in it. I was a bit surprised to see that a number of the seats were filled by other students, wearing headphones and looking at video screens, their fingers poised over keyboards. I recognized Curtis and

Gleeson, those two goons, lavatory defenders of the faith. They didn't notice my arrival.

I was ushered to a seat. Tulane tapped some keys and the screen lit up.

The challenge is yours.

"Just follow the prompts," Tulane said.

It was less intimidating than I'd expected, really. Some kind of intelligence test was first. Endless questions about all kinds of things. It was a strange mix of factual information and the kind of dumbed-down mumbo jumbo that showed up on our phones and that teachers rattled off in our classes. It wasn't that hard to come up with the answers I assumed they wanted to hear. And then there were the questions about the rules. Pretty simple, really. Multiple choice. I didn't really see how it was determining my level of intelligence. But it was just a game, right? Yet another game with rules. And I was learning to be a really good player.

After about two hours I was allowed to take a break. I headed for the bathroom and was barely in the door when Ming pushed his way in behind me and nervously shoved me into a bathroom stall. "How is it going?" he asked.

"Okay, I think."

"Gina and I already passed. We're in line for the next step."

"That's great."

"You can do this, Blake. We want you on board with us."

"I think I did okay on the IQ thing. What happens when I go back?"

"Psych tests then. Poly tomorrow, probably. But you won't hear the results for a few days. If you pass, you get your own twenty-four hours of private induction training. You'll have to give your parents a heads-up. But you can't tell them the truth about why you are doing this."

"I think they'd understand."

"Don't tell them. Even if you trust them. Because if you get found out, they might end up in trouble too."

"What happens to me if I get found out?"

Ming shook his head. "Just don't get found out."

Chapter Ten

Ming coached me some more for the lie detector test. Miss Jamieson also took me aside one day at school to ask about my progress and to remind me of the basics. No eye movement. No involuntary clues. Keep cool. Go to that happy place. It felt good to have the support and know I was part of something important. Something that went against the horrible new system that ran schools and, as I was now learning, just about everything else.

I took the polygraph test. It wasn't administered by Tulane, but by a young guy with a shiny face, a fake smile and yellow teeth. He rattled off questions. I answered. Cool as a cucumber. While he was asking, I was sailing the south seas. No one ever told me the results, but I guessed I had passed. Later that day I got a message on my phone.

Thursday 8 a.m. Eat before you come. Tell your parents. 24 hours. Be prepared.

That was it. This was really going to happen.

After school Ming and Gina found me as I walked home. They had their phones in shields, heads up to watch for what authorities now called "safety cams" on the power poles.

"Thursday," I said. "Eight a.m."

Gina nodded. "Me too."

"Not me," Ming said. "I told them I wasn't feeling well. So they've scheduled me for a week later."

I looked at Ming. Was he copping out? Suddenly I felt a whole lot less confident about our plan.

"I don't know if I'm ready for this either," I admitted.

"No, it's not like that," Gina said, guessing the source of my hesitation. "Ming and I decided one of us has to hang back as a kind of control. Like, if we both come out of this twenty-four-hour thing really shaken up, Ming will be there to help."

Her words made me even more nervous.

I guess Gina could read my face. "But don't worry," she said. "Vanessa had some advice on how to get through this next stage. We'll talk about it before Thursday."

"Who's Vanessa?" I asked.

"Miss Jamieson. She told me to call her Vanessa... but not in school."

"Well, she was right about the psych test and the poly," Ming said. "She knows what she's talking about, and she's coached others before."

I shrugged. "Okay. We all got this far. I guess we just keep going."

I tried to bullshit my parents about why I wanted to go through induction. Why I wanted to be a teacher— or the new version of a teacher. My mom saw right through it. "You don't really want to be like one of them, Blake. Don't give me that crap." Good ol' Mom.

So I told them about the Dogs, and the preparation Gina and I had done to get through the training.

"I've got a bad feeling about this," my dad said. "My own 'counselors' have been telling me about the training weekends they have in store for us. I have to participate if I want to get a job. But I don't like it. Don't let them mess with your head."

"I won't," I said. "You guys trained me well. Mind and body. All those days at sea. On duty at night for hours in the darkness. I can do this. I see it as a challenge."

In the end, I half convinced them. Truth was, they were both still in shock about having returned to a world none of us understood.

Chapter Eleven

Thursday rolled around. I ate a big breakfast. I walked to school. I reported to the office. I was asked to put my wallet, watch, belt and, yes, even my phone in a plastic bag that was sealed and put in a drawer. It seemed like a scene from one of the prison movies I had watched.

Gina was already there. We'd agreed not to even look at each other. Cameras were on us. Someone was gathering information. There were maybe ten others waiting. Then Miss Jamieson walked in. Vanessa. She looked at all of us, her face expressionless. Then she left.

One by one we were led down the hall. Then it was my turn. Shiny Boy from the poly test was my escort. He didn't smile or speak. Just nodded.

Was I scared? No. But that was because I had blocked that emotion, just as Vanessa had told me to do. Just as Ming had coached me. Time to see if I could maintain the block.

The door opened. I walked in. Shiny Boy looked me in the eye for the first time, but I couldn't read the look. A smile? A fake smile? Was it a good-luck smile or a smile that said, *Sucker*. I'd never know. It was showtime.

The door closed, and the light began to dim ever so slowly. I tried to get my bearings. Gray concrete floor, empty walls, white ceiling. The door— gray metal—with a keypad. I took a deep breath.

Antiseptic smell. Maybe some other chemical smell. I couldn't place it.

And then it went dark. Real dark. Impossibly dark. Absolutely no light, not even under the door. Black, empty space. All mine for the next twenty-four hours. And if I could pass this insane test, then what? And what if I didn't pass? What if I couldn't handle the isolation?

I waited for the hum of ventilation and that almost imperceptible sound of voices I'd heard before during punishment. But this was different. No light and no sound. At all.

I told myself that I could handle it, I really could. But the overwhelming black, with eyes open or closed, made me realize how little I had ever experienced of real darkness.

I stood upright and remained very still at first. Then I sat down on the cold concrete floor. *Just get through this and move on,* I told myself. But move on to what? I wasn't sure. Following Gina and Ming and joining the

Dogs? Infiltrating the system, the school? The rebel in me felt the power in that move. It felt like the right thing to do. I thought about my parents—fed up with materialism and jobs they hadn't liked. Dropping everything and sailing away for a break from it all. It had been such a big mistake to come back.

It was time to go to the visualization again. The boat. The sea. The sky. To go there in my head. My ultimate happy place.

If I'd still had my watch, I would at least have been able to chart the passage of time. But here in this place of almost complete sensory deprivation, I had absolutely no sense of time. I can do this, I kept telling myself. But for how long, I didn't know.

And then something in my head began to shift. A voice started saying, *No, I can't do this. I hate what's happening to me.* The voice grew louder, and then I couldn't tell if it was me actually speaking or if it was just in my head or if it was coming from someplace else.

The dark. The silence. The cold.

But it wasn't really that cold. It was the floor I was sitting on that was cold. I tried to stand and was shocked when I fell over. So I just lay there on the cold, hard floor. I felt a wave of panic rising inside me. I couldn't envision the boat or the sea anymore. Only dark.

And then I felt a kind of terror overtake the panic. I felt like there were creatures here with me. No. Not felt. I could see them. Hideous things I hadn't encountered since having nightmares as a little kid.

And then sounds. Horrible noises.

I shook my head. I sat upright again. Took a deep breath. And they went away.

As I took more deep breaths and practiced the meditation steps Ming had taught me, I could reconnect with the quiet center in my brain. But it slipped away just as quickly as it came, and I began to ask myself why this isolation routine was necessary.

Was it a test or a first step in some kind of mind-control regimen?

If it was a test, I was determined to pass it. But what if they got to me, got to Ming and Gina, and none of us came out of this unchanged?

I decided my best defense was to fall asleep.

Easier said than done. The monsters of my childhood imagination returned. I could see them, and then I could hear them. And I thought I heard screaming. From students in the other rooms? Or just in my head? I didn't know.

Was I suddenly hungry? *Yes.* Thirsty? *Yes.* No, I wouldn't die of hunger or thirst. But I might yet go crazy. *No, Blake, hold it together.*

The madness came and went. The monsters of my imagination grew louder, more vivid, more horrible. Eyes closed or open. They were still there. Until I finally mustered the strength to will them to go away.

But my thoughts were a complete jumble now. Like some other force had taken over my brain. None of what I was thinking made any sense.

And then the strangest thing happened.

The door opened and slammed back against the concrete wall. The sound ripped through my skull. The light hurt my eyes.

"Pendleton," a man's voice said. "Out."

I had a hard time focusing, but I saw Shiny Boy coming toward me. He grabbed me by the shirt, tugged me to my feet and pulled me out the door. The sudden bright light was blinding me.

Was that it? Twenty-four hours done? But why the harsh voice? The pulling and shoving? In a few seconds I was out in the hallway and blinking at the lights in the ceiling. "It's all over, Pendleton." The voice now was Tulane's. His henchman was shoving me down the hall. If I could have made my legs work better, I would have shoved back.

And run. But my brain was still fuzzy. My legs were like rubber.

"What did I do?" I croaked.

"Jamieson told us all about you," Tulane said.

"Jamieson?"

"She told me everything," he said, and then I was shoved into yet another room. Not dark but lit up by a giant white screen on one wall. The door closed quickly and solidly behind me, and I realized I was not alone. Gina was huddled on the floor. I stumbled toward her and sat down.

"Vanessa turned us in," she said. "She's not one of us. She's one of them."

"Are you all right?"

"I think so. But I don't know what's happening."

Any minute I expected the lights to go out again. Instead images began to flash on the screen. These were real. Not imagined. Images of war, violence, faces filled with hatred, fear. And then the sound came up. Loud noises. Shouting. Screaming. New horrifying images appeared on the screen faster and faster.

"Look away," Gina said. But as soon as she said it, the images appeared on all four walls, pulsating along with the terrible sounds of human suffering.

We'd gone from training to punishment. Training had seemed quite terrible, but this was much worse. Sensory overload of horrible things that no one should have to endure. I stood up and walked to the door. It was locked. The keypad on the door handle had the numbers one through nine. I started punching the keys in random order, praying I'd somehow stumble onto the exit code. No luck. No way.

Gina came and took my hand and pulled me back onto the floor. We were both kneeling now, facing each other. She pulled my forehead to hers and spoke, trying to say something reassuring.

But her words were drowned out by the screaming coming from hidden speakers.

I looked up for just a second and thought I saw a split-second image of a tree—the hemlock tree from the park. It appeared and then disappeared just as quickly. I pointed to the screen, and Gina looked up. I whispered, "Did you see something?"

The tree appeared again, ever so briefly. "Yes." Then more screaming, more horror. But then the tree appeared once more. With a number on it. Seven. *What the hell?*

More war. More violence. More contorted faces. Then the tree again. And a numeral two. Each time it appeared, another number was there on the trunk. Eight. Four. Three.

Gina whispered in my ear. "Ming," she said.

"How?" I asked.

"Not now," she said. And then the numbers stopped.

"The code is 72843," she whispered as she grabbed my hand and pulled me up. She led me to the door and punched the numbers into the keypad on the door handle.

At first nothing.

Then a click.

The door opened.

We ran.

Shiny Boy was there in the hallway blocking us, and I threw myself at him like a football lineman. I hit him low and I hit him hard. Once he was down, I saw others coming toward us, but Gina had me by the hand as we raced down the hall.

We ran as hard as we could. The hallway was filled with kids changing classes. Just going through their normal routines. It was crowded, and whoever was chasing us quickly fell behind in the mob as we wove our way through the crowd.

An alarm sounded as we left the building. "We have to get away from the cameras," Gina said, breathless.

I could hardly catch my breath. I was scared. And I knew we could never go back into that building. "The park," Gina said. "Ming will be there waiting."

I didn't realize how out of shape I was. Gina ran like lightning. I tried my best to keep up, but she had to keep stopping to wait for me. The look on her face told me this whole thing was much more serious than I had imagined. *What happens if they catch us?* I wanted to ask. *What do we do now?* But Gina was on the move again. I had to keep up.

As we ran, she kept pointing at the cameras mounted on buildings and streetlamps. We did our best to dodge around them, but we knew there was surveillance everywhere. When had that happened? Eyes on your every move? How had people let this happen?

The park. The hemlock tree. No sign of Ming. I followed Gina to the tree, and she knelt down behind it. For a weird instant I thought she was about to pray.

Instead she began to dig into the dirt at the base of the tree. She scooped out a small metal box and opened it. Inside was an old-style flip phone like the one my parents had given me when I was a little kid. It had been old and out of date even then. The other kids with their smartphones had laughed at me when I used it to call home.

Gina flipped the phone open and punched in some numbers. I was still trying to catch my breath as I looked over my shoulder to see if anyone had followed us. No one on the sidewalks. Lots of cars on the street. Heavy traffic.

And then I saw him. Ming. Sprinting through the speeding cars. Drivers were blowing their horns. One car screeched to a halt as he slammed his hand on the hood. He almost got nailed by a pickup truck and an SUV before he made it across the street and onto the sidewalk. Then he was on the grass, racing our way.

Gina pocketed the phone and stood up. "Thank God," she said when he reached us.

"No, thank Ming," he said with a cheeky grin.

My brain was racing. All along I'd had a nagging voice in my brain saying I was in way over my head. Who were we to think we could buck this system?

"Thanks for the code," Gina said. "How'd you pull that off?"

"I hacked the system, of course. But remember, that's why I didn't join you. One of us had to keep an eye on things. That would be me. I figured out how to hack the program. Just enough to get you out of there. But I had no idea that Vanessa Jamieson was one of them."

"Where can we go?" Gina asked. "Safe house in the mountains? I'm not even sure we can find it. And it's a long way off. How would we get there without being detected?"

"I'm not even sure it's there," Ming said. "Maybe Jamieson made it up. Or it's a trap. I've lost contact with the other Dogs so can't confirm anything."

"Then we're screwed," Gina said.

Chapter Twelve

"Gina, hand me the phone," I said.

She gave me a puzzled look and clutched it to her chest.

"Trust me," I said. How could she think I was going to turn us in?

Ming nodded and shrugged. Gina handed me the phone. I quickly keyed in two words.

Blue Dolphin

And then I punched in my mom's cell-phone number.

Ming and Gina were watching. "It's the name of our boat," I explained. "But we need to move."

And move we did. I knew the stream at the back of the park would lead us to the harbor. It would be a long hike, and there was a good chance we'd be detected by some form of surveillance, but I figured it was our only chance.

When I saw the boat, my heart leaped up in my throat. I saw my parents' car parked on the street nearby as we made our way through the traffic to the dockside. *Blue Dolphin* was attached to the wharf with a heavy metal chain I hadn't seen before. That didn't look good.

Then I saw my mom waving to us from inside the cabin. She was motioning for us to come on board. But as I scanned the dock area, I noticed the safety cam posted nearby. No way would we get on board without being seen. My mom kept waving.

Then I saw my dad on deck with a really big pair of bolt cutters.

He struggled mightily at first, but then he did it. He snapped the chain and tossed it into the water. My mom looked frantic now as she waved at us again. I didn't see that we had any choice.

"C'mon," I said. "I guess this is it."

The three of us ran to *Blue Dolphin*. I was certain we'd be seen. I knew we'd never get away with this. As we boarded, my father was having a hard time starting the engine. We hardly ever used it, as we tried to power by sail most everywhere. The engine finally sputtered, then caught. But we were still at dockside.

As we crowded into the cabin, I pointed to the surveillance camera on the nearby pole. "What about that?" I asked my mom.

She pointed at my father, who was standing in front of the wheel in the cabin. "Your father took it out with a rock."

"I played a lot of baseball as a kid in the old days," he said. "I still have a good arm."

"How did you know we were in trouble?" I asked. "I only sent the name of the boat."

"We were quite puzzled by your text. We knew something was up. And then the police came. They came looking for you. It sounded serious."

I saw Ming pulling his phone from his pocket. His freephone. It looked like he was about to pull it out of its shielded case. If he did that, we'd be located in no time.

"What are you doing?" I demanded.

"Look, I don't think you guys are going to make it out of here. I'm going to go back. I'll get somewhere away from here and then turn this damn thing on and let them find me. Maybe it'll give you enough time—I don't know."

"No, I'll go," Gina said. "Give me the phone."

That's when I spotted my father's little white toy—his drone camera, the one that had provided all those wonderful images I looked at each night before I went to sleep. The record of our life at sea. I picked it up and showed it to Ming.

He looked at it and smiled. "Maybe. Maybe not." He held out his phone. Without the case it would weigh next to nothing.

My father opened a drawer and grabbed wire and tools. "Go for it," he said.

Ming had no trouble creating a harness for the phone, and he kept the phone safely in its shield. "I'm going take this a few blocks over to High Street, then turn on the phone and send it off. It should circle until the battery runs out." He stood up and was about to leave the cabin when Gina stopped him.

"Look, I'm the runner here," she said. "Give me ten minutes. If I don't come back, leave without me." She grabbed the drone and Ming's phone and bolted before any of us could discuss it.

As the engine idled, my father checked over some things on the boat. My mom undid the two remaining ropes that had moored the boat to the dock. And we waited. My father took out his binoculars and scanned the skies. After a several long minutes he smiled and handed me the binoculars.

"Holy shit," I said. "There's the drone."

A few more minutes went by, and there was no sign of Gina. We waited.

And we waited some more. No one said a word.

The minutes stretched out, and the waiting was killing me. We couldn't just leave Gina behind at this point. But if we waited much longer, we stood a good chance of being found out—of being caught. And then what? God only knew what kind of punishment might be in store for all of us.

My dad lifted the binoculars and scanned the streets. He was holding his breath.

"There," he finally said, handing me the binoculars again.

Then I saw Gina, pelting along with that runner's stride that ate up the pavement. She was running like the wind, and other people on the street weren't even paying her any mind.

When she made it back to the boat, she jumped and threw herself down on the deck, breathless and sweaty. Then Dad hit the throttle, and *Blue Dolphin* pulled away from the wharf, the motor thrumming under our feet.

Ming sat down on the deck by Gina and put his arm around her. I wanted to say something to them about their parents. I wanted to know what they were thinking. Would they ever see them again? But it wasn't a time for words. Maybe once we knew we were safe, we could talk about a plan to reunite them.

My own parents were standing side by side, Mom now steering the boat as we cruised past the breakwater and headed out into the open ocean. I knew we had only a limited supply of gas. Soon we'd have to set the sail and take our chances with the wind and tide. Or take our chances with whoever might come looking to find us before we were in international waters.

But we'd made it this far, hadn't we? And I had a good feeling about our future. It felt like the rules had changed again. This time in our favor.

Jake tries to help his friend Maria after her parents are deported.

Jackson gets in over his head when he tries to save a girl from her drug-dealer boyfriend.

orca soundings

For more information on all the books

in the Orca Soundings line, please visit

orcabook.com.

Lesley Choyce is an award-winning author of more than 100 books of literary fiction, short stories, poetry, creative nonfiction, young adult novels and several books in the Orca Soundings line. His works have been shortlisted for the Stephen Leacock Medal for Humour, the White Pine Award and the Governor General's Literary Award, among others. Lesley lives in Nova Scotia.